The Wonders of Magicland

CMCM for Kids

Chud McManus

Published by Sheldon Hampstead, 2023.

Table of Contents

For Susie,

Mum & Dad love, and miss you so much

You will be in our hearts forever

The Wonders of
Magicland

by Chud McManus

The Wonders of Magicland

IN THE QUAINT VILLAGE of Brookville, where life was predictable, and the most exciting event was the annual pie contest, young siblings Jake and Emma often dreamt of adventures beyond their backyard.

One sunny day, while playing hide and seek, Emma stumbled upon a peculiar-looking key, adorned with sparkling gems and bearing the inscription "MagicLand." Without a second thought, Jake inserted the key into their garden shed door, turning it cautiously. To their astonishment, the door opened to reveal not rakes and pots, but a shimmering portal.

Taking a deep breath and holding hands, they stepped through, finding themselves in MagicLand—a realm where the impossible was every day. The ground was carpeted with rainbow grass, trees bore fruits of gold and silver, and the sky was a dance of ever-changing colours.

Their first encounter was with a talking fox named Felix, wearing a dapper suit and monocle. "Ah, newcomers!" he exclaimed. "Welcome to MagicLand, where your wildest imaginations come to life."

Jake and Emma soon discovered that MagicLand was a place of endless wonders. They sailed on candy cane boats over lakes of liquid chocolate, soared high on the backs of book-loving dragons, and even attended a school where subjects included Cloud Painting and Stardust Spells.

The most enchanting spot was the Dreamer's Den—a vast library where stories weren't just read but lived. With the help of magical spectacles, the children dived into tales of pirates, jungles, and cosmic adventures.

Yet, MagicLand wasn't without its challenges. The siblings encountered riddles that needed solving and mischievous sprites that loved playing pranks. But with every challenge, Jake and Emma learned valuable lessons about courage, friendship, and the power of imagination.

Days felt like minutes, and soon, it was time to return to Brookville. Felix approached them, offering a small bag. "Seeds from MagicLand," he explained. "Plant them in your world, and let the magic grow."

Back home, Jake and Emma transformed their once ordinary garden into a mini MagicLand, with rainbow roses and silver-leafed trees. The seeds not only brought colours but also laughter, joy, and a touch of wonder to the folks of Brookville.

And so, in a village where pies were once the highlight, tales of Jake, Emma, and the wonders of MagicLand became the Favorite bedtime story—reminding every child and adult that magic isn't just in far-off lands but can be found and nurtured right where you are.

The Box of Magic Crayons

IN THE HEART OF A SLEEPY town named Littledale, inside a quirky little shop with a crooked sign reading "Mysteries & Wonders," a box of crayons sat waiting for its next owner.

One sunny Saturday, a girl named Mia wandered into the shop with her allowance burning a hole in her pocket. The store was full of peculiar items, like clocks that ran backward and teacups that giggled when filled. But Mia's gaze landed on the box of crayons. It wasn't the largest or the shiniest item, but it was definitely the most colourful.

The shopkeeper, an elderly man with a beard that reached his knees, saw her interest and said, "Ah, those aren't just any crayons. They are magic crayons! Every drawing you make will come to life for a single day."

Mia's eyes sparkled. "Really?"

With a nod from the shopkeeper and a handful of coins from Mia, the crayons were hers.

Once home, Mia wasted no time. She drew a radiant sun in her backyard, and instantly, the gloomy day transformed into a bright, warm afternoon. Excitedly, she sketched a playful puppy, and in a burst of colour, a bouncy little dog appeared, wagging its tail.

Mia spent the whole day drawing: a slide made of rainbow, shoes that danced on their own, and a giant talking cupcake named Mr. Sprinkles. She and Mr. Sprinkles shared jokes and giggles, while the dancing shoes performed a show.

But Mia's masterpiece was yet to come. That night, with the silver crayon from the box, she drew countless stars and a gleaming moon on her bedroom ceiling. As she lay in bed, the room was filled with a soft glow, and the stars twinkled, creating a magical lullaby that danced her to sleep.

The next morning, Mia woke up to find her room back to its normal state. The puppy, the rainbow slide, Mr. Sprinkles, and even the twinkling stars had vanished, just as the shopkeeper said they would.

However, instead of being sad, Mia felt grateful for the most magical day of her life. And while the magic crayons' effects lasted only a day, the memories and joy they brought would stay with her forever.

From then on, Mia visited the "Mysteries & Wonders" shop often, always ready for her next magical adventure. And the shopkeeper would always greet her with a smile, knowing that in the hands of a child with imagination, the possibilities were endless.

And so, in Littledale, magic was just a drawing away.

The Tale of Grizzle Bear and Sunny Bunny

IN THE HEART OF WHISPERING Woods, there were two unlikely neighbours: Grizzle Bear, a gruff old bear with a frown that rarely turned upside down, and Sunny Bunny, a cheerful rabbit with a bounce in her step and a song on her lips.

One day, while Grizzle was taking his afternoon nap, Sunny Bunny decided to surprise her friend by planting some flowers outside his cave. She thought the bright blossoms would bring a smile to Grizzle's face.

However, while digging, Sunny accidentally knocked over Grizzle's Favorite honey pot, smashing it to pieces. The noise woke Grizzle, and seeing his beloved pot in ruins, he roared in anger, "Look what you've done!"

Sunny Bunny's ears drooped, her joy replaced with guilt. "I'm so sorry, Grizzle," she whispered. "I wanted to surprise you with flowers, but I made a mess instead."

Grizzle, still upset, grumbled and retreated into his cave, leaving Sunny Bunny teary-eyed.

Over the next few days, Sunny Bunny thought hard about how to make things right. She began gathering honey from the highest trees and the deepest meadows, determined to refill a new honey pot for Grizzle.

One morning, with her surprise ready, she approached Grizzle's cave and presented him with the most golden, delicious honey he'd ever seen, contained in a beautifully crafted pot.

Grizzle looked at Sunny Bunny's hopeful eyes and the effort she had put into fixing her mistake. His heart melted. "Oh, Sunny," he sighed, "it's not about the honey or the pot. It's about understanding and forgiveness."

Sunny Bunny nodded, "I understand that mistakes happen. I'm sorry for what I did, but I also hope you can see the love behind my actions."

Grizzle Bear smiled, a genuine smile, full of warmth. "And I forgive you, Sunny. Compassion and understanding are sweeter than any honey."

From that day on, Grizzle and Sunny shared many sunny afternoons, sipping honey and admiring the blossoming flowers outside the cave. The Whispering Woods echoed with tales of a bear and a bunny, teaching everyone that with a little compassion and forgiveness, even the biggest misunderstandings could lead to the sweetest friendships.

Lulu's Dream Zoo

LULU ALWAYS LOVED BEDTIME, not just because of the warm blanket or the cozy stories, but because every night she journeyed into the realm of dreams. And one night, she found herself in the most enchanting place she had ever imagined: her very own zoo.

But this was no ordinary zoo. Instead of lions or zebras, the enclosures were filled with creatures Lulu had never seen before, creatures from the farthest corners of imagination.

First, there was a "Fluffernox," a creature with the body of a fox and feathers as soft as clouds. It fluttered around playfully, letting out giggles instead of growls.

Next, she saw a "Glimmerfish" that swam in mid-air, leaving a trail of rainbow sparkles. It had fins like delicate butterfly wings and loved to hum enchanting melodies.

In the vast grassy plains, Lulu spotted "Grasselope" — a majestic deer-like creature with blades of grass as its fur. When it moved, tiny flowers blossomed beneath its hooves.

She giggled when she came across a "Choco-monkey," a mischievous monkey that swung from trees dripping with chocolate syrup and had a fur made of cotton candy.

Lulu felt an immediate bond with these fantastical creatures. It was as if they had always been waiting for her to care for them. She fed the Glimmerfish with dreams and aspirations, combed the Fluffernox with wishes, and played chase with the Grasselope under a sky painted with auroras.

As Lulu wandered deeper into the zoo, she encountered a creature that looked lost and scared. It was a "Shiverling," a creature that shimmered like the night sky, but it was cold and seeking warmth. With her innate kindness, Lulu embraced it, wrapping it in her dreamy warmth until it sparkled with happiness.

Every moment was a discovery, a joy. Lulu felt proud, connected, and deeply responsible for her magical menagerie.

But as with all dreams, dawn began to break. The fantastical creatures gathered around Lulu, each offering her a small token: a feather, a melody, a blossom, a sweet treat, and a shimmering star. They were gifts of gratitude, tokens to remember them by.

As Lulu awoke, she clutched her pillow, her heart brimming with love and wonder. Her room was the same, but the tokens from her dream animals glimmered on her bedside table, making her wonder if it was just a dream after all.

Every night, Lulu eagerly dove into sleep, hoping to return to her Dream Zoo. And while not every dream took her there, the nights that did were always magical, filled with adventure, kindness, and the wildest of wonders.

Timmy's Tiny Dinosaur

TIMMY'S FAVORITE PASTIME was digging in his backyard, hoping to uncover buried treasures. Most days, he'd find interesting rocks, old coins, or the occasional lost toy. But on one particularly sunny afternoon, he found something that made his heart race with excitement—a tiny, living dinosaur.

It was no bigger than Timmy's hand, with scaly green skin, bright yellow eyes, and a long, swishy tail. It let out a soft roar, sounding more like a kitten's meow than a mighty dinosaur's bellow.

Timmy named him "Rexie."

Having read numerous books about dinosaurs, Timmy knew he had a unique responsibility on his hands. He created a habitat for Rexie, using a large shoebox, some fresh grass, and a small bowl of water. But as the days went by, Rexie began to grow. Not too big, just enough that the shoebox wasn't enough anymore.

Timmy then built a tiny dino-park in a corner of his backyard, complete with a mud pool, a miniature jungle of potted plants, and tiny caves made from stones.

Rexie's Favorite activity was playing fetch. Yes, a dinosaur that loved fetch! He'd chase after small pebbles Timmy threw, bringing them back with a joyful hop.

But there were challenges too. Like the day Rexie tried to play with the neighbour's cat or the time he took a liking to Timmy's mom's vegetable garden. Through all the mischief and adventures, Timmy learned the importance of patience, care, and understanding.

Word of the tiny dinosaur spread, and kids from all around the neighbourhood came to see the wonder that was Rexie. Timmy, being the proud caretaker, often gave 'dino-tours,' explaining fun facts about dinosaurs and emphasizing the importance of kindness to all creatures, big or small.

One day, as Timmy sat reading a bedtime story to Rexie, he noticed a shimmer around the tiny dino. Before his eyes, Rexie transformed into a small, intricate toy dinosaur, frozen in a playful pose.

Though initially heartbroken, Timmy realized that some magic isn't meant to last forever. Rexie may have become a toy, but the lessons, joy, and memories he brought were real and everlasting.

Timmy placed toy Rexie on his bedside table, a constant reminder of their incredible time together. And as for the backyard? Well, Timmy continued his digs, always on the lookout for the next magical adventure lurking just beneath the surface.

The Cloud Jumper

SARAH HAD ALWAYS BEEN a dreamer, often found lying on her back in the meadow behind her home, gazing up at the sky. The clouds, with their ever-changing shapes, told her stories of distant lands and fantastic beasts. But on her tenth birthday, something miraculous happened. She discovered she could jump on clouds.

It started innocently. She'd taken a leap off the swing, trying to touch a particularly fluffy cloud, and to her surprise, she landed on it! It felt soft beneath her feet, like the fluffiest cotton candy, yet strong enough to hold her weight.

From that day, Sarah became the Cloud Jumper.

Each jump took her on high-flying adventures. The low-hanging cumulus clouds allowed her to bounce around her town, giving her bird's-eye views of her school, the park, and her own rooftop. The wispy cirrus clouds, high in the sky, whisked her to cooler altitudes, where she could glide over mountain peaks and sprawling forests.

But her Favorite was the majestic nimbus. Riding them, Sarah journeyed through rainstorms, feeling the exhilaration of thunder and the gentle touch of raindrops, all while safely atop her cloudy steed.

Over time, Sarah met other cloud creatures: playful cloud-pups that chased after her, graceful cloud-birds that sang harmonies with the wind, and wise old cloud-whales that told tales of the ancient skies.

With every adventure, Sarah learned something new. From the cumulus, she learned to see her world from new perspectives. The cirrus taught her to reach for great heights, no matter how unreachable they seemed. And the nimbus showed her the beauty in embracing life's storms.

But as with all magical gifts, there was a lesson to be learned. One day, eager to show her friends her cloud-jumping abilities, Sarah found that she couldn't leap onto the clouds when others were watching. It was a secret gift, meant just for her.

At first, she felt disheartened. But as she lay on the grass, watching the clouds drift by, she realized that some magic is personal, meant to teach, grow, and nurture in private. It was her way of connecting with the world, of understanding herself better.

Sarah continued her high-flying adventures, cherishing each moment and keeping the magic alive in her heart. She might not have been able to show everyone, but she could share her stories, her learnings, and the wisdom of the clouds.

Years later, as an old woman, Sarah would often be found in the meadow, her eyes reflecting the vast skies, inspiring young dreamers to look up, jump high, and chase their very own clouds.

The Day the Sun Slept In

IN THE LITTLE TOWN of Dawnsville, where mornings were greeted with golden rays and chirping birds, something very unusual happened one day. The sun...didn't rise. The hour was long past dawn, yet it remained dark as night. Birds chirped hesitantly, flowers refused to bloom, and the townsfolk, puzzled and concerned, peeked out of their curtains in disbelief.

Amidst the confusion was a young child named Leo. Curious and brave, Leo decided that if the sun wasn't going to come up on its own, he'd find a way to wake it.

He remembered a story his grandmother once told him about a silver bell that sat at the edge of the town. It was said to be a relic from ancient times, capable of reaching the ears of celestial beings.

Without a second thought, Leo set out, lantern in hand, navigating through the persistent darkness. The journey took him through the whispering woods and over the murmuring hills. As he walked, the creatures of the night, like owls and fireflies, guided his path, sensing the importance of his mission.

Finally, after what felt like hours, he reached the cliff where the legendary silver bell stood. It was large and adorned with symbols of the sun, moon, and stars. Taking a deep breath, Leo rang the bell. Its sound was deep and resonant, echoing through the stillness of the dark morning.

And then, there was a response.

A soft voice, drowsy but gentle, whispered through the darkness. "Who dares to wake me?"

"It's me, Leo," he replied. "Mr. Sun, everyone in Dawnsville is worried. Why haven't you risen today?"

There was a sigh, "Oh, Leo, I am so tired. I've risen day in and day out, without fail, for eons. Today, I just wanted to sleep in a bit."

Leo thought for a moment. "We all need rest, Mr. Sun. But so many depend on you—plants, animals, and humans alike. Could you maybe rise just for a bit, and perhaps tomorrow we can find a way to give you a longer break?"

The sun seemed to ponder this. "Promise?"

"Promise," affirmed Leo.

Slowly, a gentle glow began to emanate from the horizon. The darkness receded, unveiling a world bathed in soft, golden light. The sun, though not as bright as usual, had indeed risen.

As Leo journeyed back to town, he spread the word of the sun's weariness. The townsfolk, grateful for Leo's bravery and touched by the sun's dedication, decided to Honor the promise made.

The next day, Dawnsville remained dimly lit, with everyone using lanterns, candles, and reflective mirrors to guide their way. The sun was given its well-deserved break, rising later in the day, rejuvenated and brighter than ever.

From then on, once a year, Dawnsville celebrated "The Day of Lanterns" to remind everyone of the balance between duty and rest and to show gratitude to the tireless sun.

And Leo, he became known as the "Bringer of Light," not just for waking the sun, but for illuminating the importance of understanding and empathy in everyone's hearts.

Moon's First Day of School

FOR MILLENNIA, THE Moon watched over Earth from the sky. It saw empires rise and fall, witnessed countless sunrises, and lulled generations into peaceful slumbers. But what intrigued the Moon most were Earth's young children—with their laughter, curiosity, and boundless energy.

One day, the Moon thought, "I've seen so much, yet I know so little about these young Earthlings. Maybe I should join their school and learn directly from them."

With that, the Moon transformed itself into a childlike form—still retaining its radiant, silver glow—and gently descended to Earth.

The next morning, at Sunnyside Elementary, there was quite the buzz. Word had spread that a new student was joining, and as children gathered in the schoolyard, they gasped in wonder at the sight of the Moon, now a child, waiting by the school's entrance.

The principal, Mrs. Maple, approached, a little awestruck herself. "Welcome! You must be our new student. But, may I ask, who are you?"

"I'm the Moon," it replied with a soft, shimmering voice. "I'm here to learn about Earth's children."

A murmur of excitement spread among the students. The Moon, in their school!

The day's lessons were unlike any other. In math, the Moon learned about counting stars. In history, it was fascinated to learn how humans used its phases to tell time and mark calendars. Art class was filled with children drawing space, with the Moon right at the centre.

During recess, the Moon played hopscotch, leaping effortlessly in low gravity jumps. It joined a game of catch, where its glow made the ball easy to see, and at storytime, it shared tales of comets, galaxies, and the vast wonders of the cosmos.

But the most touching moment came during show and tell. A young girl named Lucy stood up, holding a photograph. "This is a picture of my family," she began. "We were on a late-night drive, and in the background, you can see the Moon—big and bright. My mom said it was watching over us, making sure we were safe."

The Moon, hearing this, felt an overwhelming emotion, realizing just how much it meant to the children of Earth.

As the day came to an end, the Moon, now filled with newfound knowledge and appreciation, prepared to return to the sky. The children gathered around, each offering a hug, a drawing, or a small token of friendship.

Ascending into the night, the Moon resumed its celestial form, but now it shone a little brighter, a little warmer. For within its ageless glow was the love, curiosity, and spirit of Earth's children, a bond that would last for eternity.

And down at Sunnyside Elementary, whenever children would look up at the night sky, they'd whisper, "Goodnight, Moon. See you at school tomorrow." Knowing that their celestial friend was always watching, always learning, and forever a part of their world.

Oliver's Invisible Friend

IN THE BUSTLING TOWN of Evergreen, where children played and adults were always in a hurry, Oliver was a boy with a secret. He had a friend nobody else could see—an invisible friend named Max.

Max wasn't always invisible. In a world far away, where colours sang and shadows danced, he was a radiant being of light. But one day, while exploring a mysterious portal, he found himself in Evergreen, unseen by all, except for Oliver.

To Oliver, Max was as clear as day. He had twinkling blue eyes, a mischievous grin, and a laugh that sounded like wind chimes. They became fast friends, playing hide and seek (which Max was exceptionally good at), sharing stories, and embarking on imaginary adventures.

However, while no one else could see Max, his presence wasn't entirely undetectable. When he danced, flowers would sway along, even if there was no breeze. When he laughed, leaves would rustle, and on chilly days, his warmth could be felt as a gentle, comforting embrace.

The children of Evergreen began to notice these strange occurrences. At the park, swings would move on their own, and sometimes toys would playfully hide, only to be found in the most unexpected places.

Oliver would often giggle, watching as Max played his harmless pranks. But he also felt a tad lonely, wishing others could see his incredible friend and share in the joy.

One day, during art class, Oliver had an idea. If he couldn't show Max directly, maybe he could depict him in a drawing. With bright colours and bold strokes, Oliver painted Max amidst the backdrop of Evergreen, capturing their adventures and the magic they brought.

The painting was a hit. Everyone was intrigued by Oliver's imaginary friend, who seemed to make the ordinary, extraordinary. Kids began to play along, saying "Hello, Max!" in the mornings, or offering him a seat during storytime.

It warmed Oliver's heart to see Max being accepted, even if it was in a playful, make-believe manner. And Max, although still invisible, felt seen and loved.

Time passed, and as the children of Evergreen grew, the tales of Max became legendary. Younger siblings were told stories of the invisible friend who made flowers dance and swings move on their own.

And then one day, as suddenly as he had arrived, Max was gone. Oliver, now a teen, felt his absence deeply but understood that Max had returned to his radiant world.

Evergreen moved on, but the magic of Max never truly left. For in every rustling leaf, every swaying flower, and every playful breeze, the town felt the touch of an invisible friend, reminding them always to believe in the unseen wonders of the world.

Oliver, carrying the memories of a childhood filled with magic, often gazed at the painting of Max, knowing that true friendship, whether visible or not, leaves an indelible mark on the heart.

Bella's Balloon World

IT WAS BELLA'S BIRTHDAY, and the highlight of her backyard party was a shimmering helium balloon tied with a silver string. The balloon was unlike any other—it sparkled under the sun, reflecting a rainbow of colours.

As Bella played with her friends, she couldn't help but keep one hand on her special balloon. But amidst the laughter and games, she made a wish: "I wish I could float away on an adventure!"

To Bella's astonishment, the balloon tugged her upwards, lifting her gently off the ground. Before she knew it, she was soaring above her house, her friends becoming tiny dots below. She felt a mix of excitement and fear, but the higher she rose, the more her fear faded, replaced by wonder.

Beyond the clouds, Bella discovered an astonishing world—a world where everything was floating. Houses bobbed in the air like hot air balloons, connected by swinging bridges. Trees with balloon-like canopies floated around, their roots dangling freely. Birds swam in floating water bubbles, and fish flew, gliding through the sky.

In the heart of this world was a floating market, where vendors sold their wares from hovering stalls. Bella saw children hopping from one floating platform to another, playing tag. Curious creatures, half-bird and half-fish, performed acrobatics in the air.

A kind woman, Ms. Flutter, who had wings like a butterfly, approached Bella. "You're new here!" she exclaimed. "Welcome to

Balloon World! Here, gravity isn't the boss, and everything floats with freedom."

Bella and Ms. Flutter spent the day exploring. They tasted cloud candy, played leapfrog over floating stones, and even danced on a floating stage with the stars shimmering below their feet.

But as the day neared its end, Bella began to miss her home. Sensing her feelings, Ms. Flutter said, "Remember, Bella, Balloon World is a place of dreams. If you wish to return, just hold your balloon tight and think of home."

Taking a deep breath and clutching her shimmering balloon, Bella wished to be back at her birthday party. The world around her blurred, and in an instant, she was descending, landing softly back in her backyard.

Her friends rushed towards her, awed by her sudden ascent and descent. "Where did you go?" they asked in amazement.

Bella, with a twinkle in her eye, replied, "On a floating adventure! But I'm glad to be back."

From that day on, Bella's birthday was not only remembered for cake and presents but also for her magical journey to Balloon World. And though she never left the ground again, Bella often gazed up at the sky, her heart filled with floating dreams and memories of a world where everything was free to soar.

The Whispering Woods

IN A VILLAGE NESTLED between rolling hills and vast meadows, there was a dense forest known as The Whispering Woods. Most villagers avoided it, believing it to be enchanted, but young Elara was drawn to its mysterious allure.

One day, unable to resist her curiosity, Elara ventured into the woods. The trees stood tall and majestic, their leaves rustling in a soft chorus. As she walked deeper, she began to hear faint whispers, like countless hushed voices speaking all at once.

Intrigued, Elara approached an ancient oak tree, its trunk wide and gnarled with age. She pressed her ear against the bark and listened intently.

To her astonishment, the tree began to share a tale from a time long forgotten. It spoke of days when trees walked the Earth, of magical creatures that roamed freely, and of heroes who embarked on epic quests.

For hours, Elara listened as the oak, the birches, the pines, and even the willows recounted their tales. Each tree had a unique story, a piece of history they had witnessed or been a part of.

The birch told her of a princess who once sought shelter beneath its branches, running from a dragon. The pine reminisced about snowy winters when it served as a beacon for lost travellers. The willow shared a more melancholic tale of lost love, where two lovers promised to meet under its drooping boughs but were tragically kept apart by fate.

Elara's heart swelled with emotion as she realized that these trees, often taken for granted, were living libraries, holding centuries of memories and stories.

As the sun began to set, casting a golden hue over the forest, Elara knew it was time to head home. She whispered her gratitude to the trees, promising to return and hear more of their tales.

When she emerged from The Whispering Woods, her eyes sparkled with the magic of the stories she had heard. Elara became the village storyteller, sharing the trees' tales with eager listeners around campfires and in cozy homes.

As years went by, The Whispering Woods lost its foreboding reputation. Instead, it became a place of wonder and wisdom, where children and adults alike would come, pressing their ears to the trees, listening to the ancient tales of magic, adventure, love, and loss.

And so, in a village once wary of an enchanted forest, a bridge was built between the past and the present, all thanks to a young child named Elara, who took the time to listen.

Ella's Ever-Changing Hat

IN THE HEART OF THE town of Wonderville, young Ella owned a hat that was the talk of the town. It wasn't because it was the most fashionable or the most expensive, but because it was ever-changing.

On Monday, as Ella stepped out to go to school, her hat transformed into a bird's nest, complete with chirping baby birds waiting for their morning worm. By afternoon, it had morphed into a wide-brimmed sun hat with glowing sunflowers that brightened up the classroom.

Tuesday saw the hat become a miniature aquarium. Tiny, colourful fish swam around its circumference, and Ella felt like she was carrying a piece of the ocean on her head.

As the week progressed, the hat showcased a myriad of wonders. It became a swirling galaxy of stars on Wednesday, a fluttering butterfly garden on Thursday, and a musical ensemble of drums and cymbals on Friday.

Ella never knew what to expect, but she wore the hat with pride and joy, delighting in its surprises. The hat, in return, seemed to feed off her positivity, becoming more imaginative and vibrant with each transformation.

Of course, there were challenges. Like the time her hat turned into a rain cloud and drenched her math homework. Or when it became a beehive (friendly bees, thankfully!) during a spelling test. But Ella took it all in stride, finding humour and magic in every situation.

The children in Wonderville were initially bewildered, but soon, they looked forward to seeing Ella's hat's daily transformation. It became a beloved ritual, a moment of shared wonder and anticipation.

One day, curious about the hat's origins, Ella's friend, Lucas, asked, "Where did you get such a magical hat?"

Ella smiled, "It was my grandmother's. She always said that life was full of surprises, and with this hat, every day truly is!"

Time passed, and Ella grew older. The day came when she felt it was time to pass on the hat. She gave it to a young child in Wonderville who had the same sparkle in her eyes.

And so, the magic continued, reminding everyone in Wonderville of the wonders that could be found in the everyday, in the unexpected, and in the joy of imagination. All thanks to Ella and her ever-changing hat.

Raindrop Race

ON A STORMY DAY IN the town of Rivertown, siblings Jamie and Lily were cooped up indoors. The rain poured outside, its rhythmic patter creating a soothing background tune. But indoors, restlessness bubbled as the children sought ways to entertain themselves.

Lily stared at the window, watching as raindrops slid down the glass. "Hey, Jamie," she called out, pointing to two raindrops that were nearly level with each other, "Which one do you think will reach the bottom first?"

Jamie squinted, choosing his raindrop. "I pick the one on the left. It looks faster!"

Lily giggled, "Well, then I choose the right one! Let the raindrop race begin!"

The two drops seemed to sense their challenge. They wiggled and jiggled, making their descent down the window pane. Sometimes one would surge ahead, only to be overtaken by the other a moment later. As they raced, Jamie and Lily cheered, shouting words of encouragement.

But then, something unexpected happened. The two raindrops merged into a bigger drop, speeding down together.

The siblings looked at each other in surprise. "It's a tie!" Jamie exclaimed.

Lily nodded, smiling. "They decided to join forces instead of competing."

Throughout the afternoon, the raindrop races became the main event in the house. The children even started giving names to their chosen drops—like Speedy, Drizzle, and Thunderbolt. Each race was different; sometimes there were clear winners, other times more raindrops teamed up, creating larger and faster streaks.

Soon, their laughter and excitement drew the attention of their parents. To their amazement, the living room transformed into a raindrop racing stadium, with Jamie and Lily providing lively commentary.

That evening, as the storm subsided and the last rays of sunlight peeked through the clouds, the family sat down with cups of cocoa. The raindrop races were the talk of the evening, with each member sharing their Favorite moments.

Jamie turned to Lily, "You know, at first I was upset about being stuck indoors. But thanks to our raindrop races, this turned out to be one of the best days ever!"

Lily grinned, "That's the magic of imagination! It can turn any ordinary moment into an adventure."

And so, in a cozy house in Rivertown, a stormy day became a cherished memory—a day of raindrop races, family bonding, and the endless wonders of a child's imagination.

The Lost Star

ON THE EDGE OF THE sleepy town of Celestia, where nights were clear and the stars shone brightest, an extraordinary event occurred. A young star, twinkling with a golden glow, fell from the sky, landing softly in the town's central park.

The next morning, siblings Nora, Max, and little Elsie discovered the star while playing. It was no bigger than a soccer ball, pulsating with a gentle warmth and emitting a soft, melodic hum.

Nora, ever the protective older sister, cautioned, "We need to be careful. It's lost and far from home."

Max, full of curiosity, added, "It's a star! How did it even fall? And how can we help it get back?"

The young star, sensing their kind intentions, projected images into the children's minds. They saw vast galaxies, swirling nebulae, and a shining constellation shaped like a swan—its home.

Understanding the star's plea, the trio decided to help. But the challenge was significant. How does one return a star to the sky?

The children tried various methods. They used a trampoline, hoping to bounce the star back into space. They attempted to construct a giant slingshot, and even contemplated climbing the town's tallest tree to get it closer to its celestial home. But all efforts were in vain.

Desperate, little Elsie whispered into the star's glowing surface, "Don't worry, we'll find a way."

That night, as the children camped beside the star, guarding and comforting it, the park was filled with a mysterious glow. Moths, fireflies, and even curious nocturnal animals gathered, drawn by the star's enchanting light.

Then, in the midnight hour, the town's elderly astronomer, Mr. Lumina, approached. Having heard tales of the fallen star, he brought with him an ancient telescope, ornate and inscribed with cosmic symbols.

"Legends speak of stars that sometimes lose their way," he began. "This telescope has magical properties. It creates a bridge between Earth and the cosmos."

Positioning the telescope to face the constellation of the swan, Mr. Lumina chanted an old stargazing hymn. A pathway of light appeared, connecting the star to its distant home.

The star floated upwards, its glow intensifying, illuminating the entire park. It paused for a moment above the children, its shimmering light enveloping them in a gentle embrace, as if saying goodbye.

With one final burst of brilliance, the star shot up, traveling the light bridge, and took its rightful place in the swan constellation.

The pathway faded, and the night returned to its peaceful serenity. The children, eyes filled with wonder, gazed at the sky, their hearts filled with pride and joy.

Mr. Lumina, packing his telescope, whispered, "Remember, every star has its place, and sometimes, all it takes is a bit of kindness, imagination, and belief to overcome the impossible."

And so, in the town of Celestia, a tale was born—a tale of a lost star, three determined children, and a night when magic bridged the Earth and the stars.

Tommy's Tickle Trunk

TOMMY WAS AN AVERAGE boy with an average life, but there was one thing extraordinary about him—his Tickle Trunk. This was no ordinary trunk; it was painted in vibrant colours, adorned with shimmering stars and mischievous smiley faces.

Every morning, before school or during a gloomy afternoon, Tommy would open the trunk, and out would pop something utterly hilarious and unexpected. It might be a rubber chicken wearing sunglasses, a joke book filled with the silliest puns, or a hat that, when worn, would play goofy music and make everyone around break into spontaneous dance.

One day, at school, Tommy noticed his friend Lucy looking downcast. Wanting to cheer her up, he decided to introduce her to the magic of his Tickle Trunk. At recess, he opened the trunk, and out flew a bunch of helium-filled balloons, each one carrying a ticklish feather. Soon, the air was filled with laughter as kids tried to catch the balloons, only to be rewarded with playful tickles.

Lucy's gloom vanished, replaced by chuckles and glee. "That trunk really is magical!" she exclaimed.

As word spread, Tommy's Tickle Trunk became the highlight of many days. Whenever someone was feeling blue or the school had a particularly tough exam, Tommy would open the trunk. Sometimes it would be a pie-in-the-face kit or shoes that squeaked like ducks. On one memorable occasion, it produced a mini circus of marshmallow animals, each performing comical tricks.

The Tickle Trunk wasn't just about laughter, though. It taught Tommy and his friends the importance of finding joy in the little things and the magic of sharing a smile. It reminded them that even on the darkest days, there's always something to chuckle about.

One day, a new student named Ryan joined the school. Coming from a different city, he felt out of place and lonely. Sensing an opportunity, Tommy brought out his Tickle Trunk. This time, it gave them a map, leading to a treasure of...giggles! They embarked on a mini-adventure, following the map's clues, each one sillier than the last, until they found a chest filled with whoopee cushions.

Ryan laughed heartily, the ice of his loneliness melting away. "Thanks, Tommy," he said, grinning from ear to ear. "This has been the best day ever."

Years passed, and as children often do, Tommy grew up. The Tickle Trunk found a new home in his attic. But its legacy lived on. Every now and then, on family gatherings or reunions, someone would mention the trunk, and the room would echo with shared laughter and cherished memories.

And so, in the pages of Tommy's life, the Tickle Trunk became a symbol—a reminder that happiness can be found in the smallest of things and that the joy of laughter is the best gift one can share.

Secrets of the Seashell

ON THE GOLDEN SHORES of Misty Beach, young Mia stumbled upon a unique seashell. Unlike the others, this one shimmered with iridescent hues of blue and purple and had an intricate spiral pattern that seemed to go on forever.

Mia, always being imaginative, placed the shell close to her ear, hoping to hear the familiar sound of the ocean. Instead, she heard a soft, melodic voice, "Whisper a wish, and dive into wonder."

Feeling adventurous, Mia whispered, "I wish to see the world inside the ocean."

Suddenly, the world around Mia began to blur. The sandy beach and the swaying palm trees faded away, replaced by a vast, vibrant underwater kingdom. The sun's rays pierced the surface, creating patterns on coral palaces and illuminating the waters.

Mia, to her amazement, could breathe and talk underwater. She was met by Selena, a mermaid with flowing silver hair and a tail that sparkled like a constellation. "Welcome to the Ocean Realm," Selena greeted, her voice like a bubbling brook.

Together, they explored this watery world. Mia rode on the backs of giant sea turtles, danced with jellyfish that lit up like lanterns, and played hide and seek amidst forests of seaweed. Schools of fish, in dazzling arrays of colours, swam around her, each introducing themselves and sharing tales of underwater adventures.

The most magical moment was at the Heart of the Ocean, a cavern where the walls were studded with pearls and gemstones. Here, Mia discovered the Ocean's Memory—a swirling vortex that showed the history of the sea, from the time of ancient leviathans to the playful dolphins of today.

As the day neared its end, Mia and Selena sat on a coral cliff, watching a mesmerizing display of bioluminescent creatures lighting up the ocean's depths. "The sea is not just about wonder," Selena whispered, "but also respect. Always remember to care for it."

As Mia nodded, holding her seashell close, the underwater realm faded, and she found herself back on Misty Beach. The seashell no longer shimmered but was just an ordinary shell. Yet, the magic it held was imprinted in Mia's heart forever.

Mia became the protector of the beach, organizing clean-ups and teaching others about the marvels of the ocean. And sometimes, when the sun set, and the waves kissed the shore, she would whisper into a seashell, thankful for her watery adventure and the lessons of the deep.

Thus, in a little town by the sea, tales of a young girl and her magical journey to the Ocean Realm became legends, reminding everyone of the wonders beneath the waves and the importance of protecting them.

The Candy Cane Forest

IN THE QUAINT VILLAGE of Sweetvale, every winter, children would bundle up, eagerly awaiting the first snowfall. For it was said that when the first snowflake touched the ground, the Candy Cane Forest would come alive.

This year, siblings Lila and Ben decided to embark on an adventure to this magical forest. As the first snow began to fall, they set off, guided by tales of their grandparents, seeking the forest where candy canes sprouted like trees and hot cocoa flowed like babbling brooks.

After a short journey, they found themselves at the forest's entrance, marked by a candy cane arch. As they stepped in, the scene before them was even more enchanting than the tales. Tall candy canes, striped in red and white, reached for the sky, their tops glistening with frost. The ground was blanketed in soft minty snow, which, when tasted, had the sweetness of sugar.

Following the cocoa's rich aroma, they came across a stream, where hot chocolate flowed, with marshmallow lilies floating atop. Nearby, peppermint fish leapt joyfully, their shiny scales reflecting the winter sun.

The heart of the forest held the grandest spectacle: The Cocoa Cascade, a waterfall where hot chocolate poured over layers of waffle-cone rocks, filling the air with a delicious warmth. By its side stood the Marshmallow Meadow, a field of fluffy, white marshmallows waiting to be picked and added to a cup of cocoa.

As Lila and Ben wandered deeper, they stumbled upon the Gingerbread Grove. Tiny gingerbread squirrels scampered around, while gingerbread birds tweeted sweet melodies from above.

The duo played for hours, sliding down candy cane slopes, building snowmen with gumdrop buttons, and sipping on the finest hot chocolate they'd ever tasted.

As the day neared its end and the sky painted hues of pink and orange, they heard a jingling sound. From the forest's depths emerged Mrs. Claus, riding a sleigh pulled by chocolate reindeer.

"Ah, young adventurers," she greeted with a twinkle in her eye. "The Candy Cane Forest is a place of joy and wonder, but remember, its magic lasts only a day."

Understanding the hint, Lila and Ben climbed onto her sleigh. With a whoosh, they soared over the forest, catching one last glimpse of its splendour.

They were dropped off just outside Sweetvale, the Candy Cane Forest fading as the last snowflake of the day settled.

Back home, the siblings shared tales of their snowy adventure, their cups filled with hot cocoa and hearts brimming with memories.

The Candy Cane Forest became their winter tradition, a magical realm they visited each year, where the wonders of the season came alive, and the spirit of joy and sharing was celebrated in the sweetest way possible.

Daisy's Dancing Shoes

IN THE ATTIC OF DAISY'S home, buried under old trunks and dusty books, lay a pair of shimmering red shoes. They once belonged to her great-grandmother, a legendary dancer in her time.

One day, while exploring, Daisy found these shoes. Intrigued, she tried them on. They fit perfectly, hugging her feet like they were custom-made for her. But the moment she stood up, a magical whirlwind enveloped her.

Suddenly, Daisy found herself in a grand ballroom, with chandeliers, gentlemen in tailcoats, and ladies in flowing gowns. The shoes started moving on their own, guiding her gracefully through a waltz. As the music swirled, Daisy danced with partners who spun her around, her feet matching their every step perfectly.

As the waltz ended, the scene shifted. Now Daisy was on a lively street in Buenos Aires. The rhythm of tango filled the air. Men and women clapped and cheered as Daisy moved passionately, her shoes capturing the essence of the dance. The cobblestone streets became her stage, and the moonlit night her spotlight.

The adventure didn't stop there. The shoes whisked Daisy away to a jazzy club in 1920s New Orleans. She tapped and twirled to the beat of live jazz, the soles of her shoes echoing the rhythm of the drums.

Next, she found herself on a sunny beach in Brazil, amidst a carnival. The shoes moved her feet to the energetic beats of samba. Dancers in vibrant costumes joined her, and they formed a parade, celebrating life and dance.

With every transition, Daisy embraced the dance of the era, instinctively knowing the moves and steps. It was as if the shoes carried the memories and skills of every dancer who'd ever worn them.

As dawn approached, Daisy finally returned to her attic, the magic of the shoes fading but the memories still vivid in her mind.

She carefully placed the shoes back into the trunk, whispering a thank you to them. For she now understood their power—to not just dance but to connect with the rhythms and stories of bygone eras.

Daisy might have returned the shoes to their resting place, but their magic lived on. She joined a dance academy, sharing her adventures and using the skills she'd learned. With every twirl and step, she honoured the legacy of the dancing shoes, ensuring that their magic and stories would continue to inspire for generations to come.

Milo and the Moon Moth

IN THE QUIET TOWN OF LunaVale, where the moon played peek-a-boo behind mountaintops, young Milo often gazed at the night sky, searching for constellations and shooting stars. One particular evening, something magical caught his eye—a soft, luminous glow moving gracefully among the trees. It was a moth, but not just any moth. It was the Moon Moth, a rare creature said to appear only once in a blue moon.

The Moon Moth landed delicately on Milo's window ledge, its wings shimmering like a tapestry of moonbeams. Sensing no harm, Milo gently extended his finger, and to his delight, the moth danced onto it.

Intrigued, Milo opened his book on nocturnal creatures and discovered that the Moon Moth was known for its unique ability to navigate using the light of the moon and stars. It was said that whoever it chose to befriend would be taken on a magical night-time adventure.

With a flutter, the Moon Moth beckoned Milo to follow. And, grabbing a jacket, he did. They ventured into the woods, where every tree, rock, and brook shimmered under the moth's radiant glow. They encountered owls, raccoons, and even a family of sleeping bears, all bathed in a gentle luminescence.

The highlight of the adventure was Moonlit Meadow—a clearing where thousands of fireflies gathered, creating a spectacle of floating lights. The Moon Moth, drawing energy from this sight, began to glow even brighter. Under its light, the meadow's flowers bloomed, revealing their hidden nighttime hues.

As dawn approached, the Moon Moth led Milo back to his home. But before it departed, it circled Milo, wrapping him in a cocoon of soft moonlight. When the light dissipated, Milo found a small, moon-shaped pendant in his hand. A gift, a keepsake, a reminder of their magical journey.

Years passed, and while Milo grew older, his memories of the Moon Moth remained vivid. He often sat on his porch, gazing at the night sky, hoping for another glimpse of his luminous friend. But the Moon Moth, true to its legend, remained elusive.

However, the moon-shaped pendant always glowed softly around Milo's neck, a beacon for all of LunaVale's creatures. They often visited him, sharing tales of their nighttime escapades, ensuring that the magic of that one special night lived on.

And so, in tales whispered from one generation to the next, the legend of Milo and the Moon Moth became an integral part of LunaVale's lore—a story of friendship, wonder, and the enchanting mysteries of the night.

The Painted Pyjamas

IN THE BUSTLING CITY of Storybrook, nestled in a little shop called "Dreamy Nights," was a special pair of pyjamas. They were painted with intricate characters—daring pirates, majestic dragons, graceful dancers, and mysterious wizards.

One evening, a young girl named Ava received these pyjamas as a gift from her grandmother. "These are no ordinary pyjamas," her grandmother whispered with a wink. "Wear them tonight, and you'll see."

Intrigued, Ava put on the pyjamas and snuggled into bed. Just as she was drifting off to sleep, she felt a gentle nudge. Startled, she opened her eyes to find the characters from her pyjamas standing on her bed, very much alive!

The pirate, with a twirling beard and a feathered hat, stepped forward. "Ahoy, Ava! Ready for an adventure on the high seas?" Before she could answer, the room transformed into a ship deck, with waves crashing and stars guiding their way. Ava, joining the pirate's crew, searched for hidden treasures and battled tempests, all while learning the true meaning of bravery.

As dawn approached, the pirate scene faded, and in its place stood a magnificent dragon. It invited Ava onto its back, and together, they soared over mystical lands, from floating islands to crystal caves. The dragon taught Ava about loyalty and the bond shared by all creatures, big or small.

The next night, Ava eagerly donned the pyjamas again. This time, a graceful dancer twirled into existence. The room became a grand ballroom, and Ava, wearing a sparkling gown, danced the waltz, the tango, and even the cha-cha. From the dancer, she learned about passion and the joy that comes from expressing oneself.

On the third night, the wise wizard, with a long silvery beard and a hat that reached the clouds, shared tales of magic. They brewed potions, cast spells, and travelled through portals to other dimensions. The wizard taught Ava about wisdom and the power of knowledge.

Each night, a new story unfolded, filling Ava's dreams with adventures, lessons, and a world of imagination.

One morning, as the sun's first rays filtered into her room, Ava noticed that the characters on her pyjamas were fading. Sad, she approached her grandmother, fearing she'd never experience the adventures again.

Her grandmother, smiling gently, said, "The pyjamas brought the stories to life, but the magic, my dear, resides in your heart. Every night, as you close your eyes, let your imagination soar. The characters may have faded, but the tales and lessons will live on in your dreams."

And so, in the heart of Storybrook, Ava became a storyteller, weaving tales of pirates, dragons, dancers, and wizards. And every night, as she drifted off to sleep in her once-painted pyjamas, she journeyed to far-off lands, proving that magic, indeed, resides in the heart of every dreamer.

The Pillow Fort Kingdom

IN A SUNNY ROOM ADORNED with colourful posters and toys, young Alex worked diligently on his masterpiece—a vast pillow fort. Using cushions, blankets, and a little bit of imagination, he created a multi-roomed castle complete with turrets and a drawbridge.

As the evening settled and the room dimmed, a curious shimmer emanated from within the fort. Drawn by the glow, Alex crawled inside and was immediately transported to a place far from his bedroom—a sprawling medieval kingdom with stone castles, bustling marketplaces, and vast fields.

To his astonishment, the townsfolk cheered upon seeing him. "The hero has arrived!" they exclaimed. A wise old woman named Elara approached Alex, her robes flowing and eyes twinkling with knowledge. "Our kingdom has been under the shadow of the Dark Sorcerer," she began. "Legends foretold of a young hero arriving from the Pillow Fort Realm to save us."

Overwhelmed but determined, Alex agreed to help. His pillow fort became his training ground. The soft cushions turned into challenging terrains, the hanging blankets transformed into mazes, and his stuffed toys became both allies and adversaries, helping him hone his skills.

With each passing day, Alex undertook quests, from retrieving magical artifacts to befriending dragons. He learned the values of courage, friendship, and perseverance. And as he grew stronger, the kingdom's hope grew brighter.

The final showdown took place atop the Moonlit Tower. The Dark Sorcerer, armed with illusions and enchantments, battled fiercely. But Alex, with his newfound skills and the support of the kingdom's inhabitants, managed to outwit and defeat him.

The dark clouds lifted, replaced by golden rays that bathed the kingdom in warmth. Alex was celebrated as the hero from the Pillow Fort Realm. Elara approached him, a tear in her eye, "You've saved us, brave hero. But now it's time to return to your world."

With a heavy heart, Alex agreed. As he stepped into his pillow fort, the kingdom began to fade, transforming back into his cozy bedroom. The adventure had felt so real, yet all that remained was the fort, his toys, and the memories.

The next morning, Alex recounted his tales to his parents, who listened with amused smiles. They might have seen it as a child's vivid imagination, but to Alex, it was a real adventure, a testament to the magic that lay within his pillow fort.

And so, in a little room filled with toys and laughter, legends were born—tales of the Pillow Fort Kingdom and a young hero named Alex, who reminded everyone that adventure, magic, and heroism could be found in the unlikeliest of places.

Lenny's Library Ladder

IN THE HEART OF A VIBRANT town, there was a grand library that stood tall and proud, holding centuries of knowledge. Lenny, a bright-eyed boy with an insatiable appetite for stories, visited this library every chance he got. Among the library's treasures was a peculiar wooden ladder, said to be as old as the library itself. Unlike the other ladders, this one had intricate carvings of various storybook characters.

One day, while reaching for a book titled "The Adventures of Pirate Pete," Lenny's hand brushed against one of the ladder's carvings—a fierce-looking pirate with a parrot on his shoulder. Suddenly, the world around him spun, and when things settled, Lenny found himself aboard a bustling pirate ship. The salty sea air, the roaring waves, and, most astonishingly, Pirate Pete himself stood before Lenny, sword in hand, welcoming him to join his crew.

Lenny's days transformed into thrilling adventures. By touching a carving and thinking of a story, the ladder transported him right into its plot. He rode with knights, outwitted cunning foxes, flew with dragons, and even attended a school of magic. Each adventure brought lessons of bravery, wisdom, friendship, and the endless bounds of imagination.

Word of Lenny's magical escapades spread among the children. The library, once a quiet place, became a hub of excitement. Under Lenny's guidance, kids embarked on their own adventures, diving into stories and emerging with wide eyes and tales of wonder.

But with every great power comes responsibility. The wise librarian, Mrs. Wren, took Lenny aside one day. "The ladder is a gift," she whispered, "but remember to always respect the stories. They are worlds in their own right."

Lenny understood. He ensured that every child who used the ladder returned the stories to their rightful places and treated the characters with kindness.

Years passed, and Lenny grew older. But the magic of the ladder remained, and it became a beacon for every child seeking adventure. Lenny often returned to the library, watching new generations climb the ladder, their faces filled with awe and anticipation.

And so, in a town that thrived on tales and imagination, Lenny's Library Ladder became legendary—a bridge between the real world and the enchanting realm of stories, reminding everyone that magic can be found on the pages of a book and in the heart of a curious child.

Adventures with Pidge Wiblet

IN THE QUIET TOWN OF Featherbrook, where days were long and nights were filled with starry skies, children whispered tales of Pidge Wiblet—the legendary bird with a cockney accent, and turbocharged speed. He was also a Ninja.

Jenny, a ten-year-old with a penchant for adventure, always hoped she'd meet Pidge. One night, as she stared out of her window, a shadowy figure swooped down, landing gracefully on her windowsill. It was Pidge Wiblet, his cool sneakers shimmering in the moonlight.

"Oi there, Jenny!" he greeted with a grin, his cockney accent unmistakable. "Fancy a trip around the universe, do ya?"

Without hesitation, Jenny climbed onto Pidge's sturdy back. With a mighty flap and a "Hold on tight!" from Pidge, they soared into the sky. Suddenly, flames burst from Pidge's bottom as they entered turbo flight speed, zipping past stars and galaxies.

Their first stop was the Moonlit Marshes of Mars. The landscape was bathed in silver, with glowing creatures illuminating the terrain. Pidge, ever the ninja, showed Jenny some stealthy moves, as they played hide and seek among the starlit reeds.

Next, they flew to the Dancing Nebula, a place where colours swirled and stars twirled. Here, Pidge tapped his sneakers, activating a rhythmic beat. Together, they danced, leaving a trail of stardust in their wake.

The adventure took a thrilling turn when they encountered space pirates trying to steal the music of the cosmos. With Pidge's ninja skills and Jenny's newfound dance moves, they outwitted the pirates, saving the universe's harmony.

As dawn approached, Pidge and Jenny returned to Featherbrook. "Remember," Pidge whispered, ruffling Jenny's hair, "adventures await when you dare to dream." He then took off into the sky, turbo speed style, smelly flames lighting up the dawn morn.

Jenny woke up thinking it was all a dream, but a pair of cool sneakers next to her bed and a note reading, "Till next time, adventurer!" confirmed the magic of the night.

From that day on, Featherbrook buzzed with tales of Pidge Wiblet and his adventures, a symbol of endless possibilities, dreams, and the magic that exists just beyond the horizon.

The Colourful Castle

IN A LAND NOT SO FAR away, atop a rolling green hill, stood the Colourful Castle. Its walls were painted every shade imaginable, from cerulean blue to sunshine yellow. The flag that flew high above the castle had stripes, spots, zigzags, and swirls, representing the diversity of its inhabitants.

King Melody and Queen Harmony ruled the land. They believed that every individual, no matter their colour, shape, or size, had a unique talent and deserved a place in the kingdom.

One sunny morning, a proclamation was announced throughout the land: "The annual Talent Fiesta is approaching! Everyone is invited to showcase their special skills!"

Creatures from all corners of the kingdom began preparing. There was Delia, a dragon who loved to dance but was always too shy because she thought her scales were too shiny. Sammy, a tiny snail who painted mini masterpieces, doubted anyone would notice his art. And then there was Luna, a lioness with a voice so soft, it was the complete opposite of a roar.

The day of the Talent Fiesta arrived. The castle grounds bustled with excitement. Delia took a deep breath and began to dance, her scales reflecting light and creating a dazzling display. The audience was mesmerized by her grace and the shimmering patterns she created.

Sammy, with a little encouragement, displayed his intricate paintings, which drew a crowd. People leaned in, marvelling at the details and the stories each painting told.

Luna, nervous but determined, sang a lullaby. Her voice, gentle and soothing, captivated everyone, proving that you didn't need to roar to be heard.

As the day ended, King Melody and Queen Harmony addressed their people. "In our kingdom, every colour, every note, and every stroke has its place. Each of you, with your unique talents, makes our land brighter and richer."

From that day on, Delia started a dance school, teaching everyone to embrace their shine. Sammy's art was displayed in the castle's grand hall, and Luna sang stories of bravery and hope every evening.

The Colourful Castle became a beacon of inclusivity, a place where differences were celebrated, and everyone had a chance to shine. And the kingdom's people lived harmoniously, knowing that when everyone is included, the world becomes a more vibrant and beautiful place.

Frank and the Whimsical Wind

In the cozy town of Littletown, children often looked up at the sky, not for birds or planes, but for Frank—the flying purple kitten. With fur as radiant as the evening sky, she was indeed a sight to behold. But what truly made Frank stand out was her tail: it had a little mouth that spoke just like a grumpy old man.

"It's too cloudy," or "Why are we going this way?" the tail would grumble, especially when Frank took her daily flights.

One sunny morning, Frank encountered Millie, a young girl with pigtails, trying to set up a lemonade stall. She looked rather distressed.

"Need some help?" Frank purred, hovering above.

Millie looked up, eyes wide in amazement. "Wow! A flying kitten! I've heard stories about you."

Frank's tail interrupted, "And I bet they all mentioned how magnificent I am."

Frank giggled, "Sorry about him. He's grumpy but means well. Now, how can we assist you?"

Millie sighed, "I wanted to make a digital payment system for my lemonade stall using this tablet, but I can't figure it out. Everyone uses digital wallets these days!"

Frank nodded, "A modern lemonade stand! I love it. Let's see." As Frank and her tail peered at the tablet, she realized she didn't know how to set it up either.

"Maybe Old Man Jenkins can help," Millie suggested, pointing to the elderly man across the street who was known for his tech-savvy ways.

Frank's tail grunted, "Hmph! What could he possibly know about modern gadgets?"

Ignoring the tail's skepticism, Frank and Millie approached Old Man Jenkins, who was more than happy to assist. Within minutes, he had set up the digital payment system, complete with a QR code and all.

Frank's tail was in disbelief. "Well, I never! An old man setting up modern tech!"

Millie laughed, "You can't judge a book by its cover—or, in your case, an old man by his wrinkles!"

Over the next few hours, Frank helped attract customers with her flying antics while Millie sold lemonade. The digital payment system was a hit! Kids loved the techy approach, and even adults appreciated the convenience.

As the sun set, painting the sky with hues of orange and pink, Millie packed up her stall. She had not only earned a decent sum but had also learned the importance of embracing both the old and the new.

Frank, preparing for her evening flight, turned to Millie, "Today was a good day. We learned something valuable."

Millie nodded, "That both tradition and innovation have their place. And together, they make things even better."

Frank's tail added, grumblingly but with a hint of a smile, "And maybe, just maybe, I shouldn't be so quick to judge."

Frank giggled, giving her tail a playful swish. "Always learning, aren't we?"

With a final wave, Frank soared into the sky, her purple silhouette a reminder of the magic that happens when the old and the new come together.

And in Littletown, as children gazed up, tales of the flying kitten and her wise old tail became legendary—a story of friendship, adaptability, and the harmonious dance between the past and the future.

Appendix

IN THE SMALL TOWN OF BodyVille, every organ and body part had its own unique job. Mr. Heart pumped away, Miss Brain always had bright ideas, and the Lungs twins, Innie and Outie, loved to breathe in fresh air.

But in a snug corner of BodyVille was Appendix. He was sort of...well, misunderstood. Nobody quite knew what his job was. The townsfolk would often scratch their heads, wondering, "What does Appendix actually do all day?"

One morning, as the sun stretched and yawned, Appendix decided he'd had enough of this identity crisis. He was going to find himself a job! First, he tried helping Mr. Heart pump. But all he managed to do was splash about, creating a ruckus.

Next, he tried to assist the Lungs twins. But every time he tried to help, he just ended up making them giggle with his hiccups.

Feeling a tad deflated, Appendix trudged along and bumped into Stomach. Seeing his downcast look, Stomach burped (which is how she usually said hello) and asked, "What's up, buddy?"

"I just want to be useful," Appendix sighed. Stomach chuckled, "Why not organize a party? We could use some fun in BodyVille."

Inspired, Appendix jumped into action. He sent out invitations (via Nerve-Express) and started preparing. He organized games, like "Tug of Intestines" and "Pass the Platelets." He even invited Gut Bacteria for some funky music.

The day of the party arrived, and it was a blast! Mr. Heart did the salsa, Kidneys juggled water balloons, and even grumpy old Liver let loose with a smile.

At the end of the day, as everyone thanked Appendix for the amazing time, Brain had a revelation. "Appendix, I think I've figured out your role in BodyVille. You remind us to relax, have fun, and not take life too seriously."

From that day on, Appendix was known as the "Party Planner of BodyVille." And while he may not have had an everyday job like pumping or thinking, he brought something equally important to the town - joy, laughter, and a reminder that sometimes, you just need to dance.

And so, in the bustling town of BodyVille, among hardworking organs and busy body parts, Appendix found his unique place - ensuring that amidst all the work, there was always time for a hearty chuckle.

Don't miss out!

Visit the website below and you can sign up to receive emails whenever Chud McManus publishes a new book. There's no charge and no obligation.

https://books2read.com/r/B-A-RJBBB-PHRPC

BOOKS2READ

Connecting independent readers to independent writers.

Also by Chud McManus

CMCM for Kids
The Wonders of Magicland

Standalone
Explore the World

About the Author

Hailing from the picturesque landscapes of Victoria, Australia, Chud's life has been nothing short of an eclectic tapestry of experiences. An alumnus of Emmanuel College, a school celebrated for nurturing the careers of acclaimed musicians, sports legends, and comedic geniuses, Chud shown an interest in, and experimented in writing but his mind was set on his other passions.

While he showed a keen interest in writing during his school years and experimented with weaving stories and songwriting, Chud humbly admits he wasn't always the best. But as they say, passion often trumps proficiency, and Chud's relentless drive for expression saw him diving into various artistic pursuits. His adolescent years painted a picture of a young man torn between the rhythmic beats of drumming for a punk band, melodious tunes of singing for another, and the adrenaline-filled kicks and punches of Muay Thai.

As adulthood dawned, Chud's empathetic nature drew him towards a career in mental health. It was here that he not only contributed to the well-being of others but also tapped into his innate gift for storytelling. Juggling between his profound profession and moonlighting as a comedian, Chud became a beacon of creativity, regaling audiences with tales birthed from his unique experiences and imagination.

Yet, life had other plans. Facing challenges with his own mental health, Chud made the heart-wrenching decision to step away from the comedy stage. But as with every obstacle he'd faced before, this too became an avenue for evolution. Chud turned to his first love, writing, channeling his trials and tribulations into words that resonated deeply with readers worldwide.

Today, Chud McManus stands tall as an accomplished writer. His works range from heartfelt creative pieces to well-researched non-fiction, shedding light on topics he holds dear. And with numerous fiction projects on the horizon, his literary journey seems boundless.

Through the multifaceted narrative of Chud's life, one can see the undying spirit of a man who, no matter the setbacks, always finds a way to translate his experiences into art, touching the souls of those who encounter his work.